Emma's Pet

Emma's Pet

by David McPhail

PUFFIN BOOKS

for Ashly Lee LaBrie

Unicorn is a registered trademark of Dutton Children's Books.
Library of Congress number 85-4414
ISBN 978-0-14-054749-8
Published in the United States by Dutton Children's Books,
a division of Penguin Books USA Inc.
345 Hudson Street, New York, New York 10014
Editor: Ann Durell   Designer: Isabel Warren-Lynch
Manufactured in China by South China Printing Co.
First Unicorn Edition 1988   COBE

22 23 24 25 26 27 28 29 30

"I want a pet," Emma told her mother one day.
"You have a pet," said her mother.

"Fluffy's not cuddly," said Emma.
"I want a big soft cuddly pet."

So Emma went looking for a pet.

The first thing she found was a bug.
Even Emma couldn't say that was cuddly.

The mouse she found was soft and cuddly,
but it wasn't big.

The bird had nice soft feathers…

but it was too busy

feeding its family to be anybody's pet.

The frog wasn't soft and cuddly,
but it might have made a good pet...

if it hadn't taken a bath with Emma's mother.

The snake she picked up was *too* cuddly for Emma.

Then she got a fish...

but that was too wet and slippery.

And the dog she brought home
already belonged to someone else.

Emma was sad.

She sat down on a rock and began to cry.

The rock moved.
It was a turtle!

But it wasn't any softer or any more cuddly than a rock.

And then Emma saw the biggest, softest,
cuddliest thing she had ever seen.

It was her father!

"Will you be my pet?" she asked.

"Always," said her father. "Will you be mine?"
"Yes," said Emma.

And she hugged her new big soft cuddly pet.
And it hugged her right back.